For the gorgeous Katinka
And for Georgie and Albie too, for putting up with me
— A.C.

To Archie Harold
With love, Harold and Jeannie
— R.A.

ISBN-13: 978-0-545-16191-6
ISBN-10: 0-545-16191-6
Text copyright © 2006 by Andy Cutbill.
Illustrations copyright © 2006 by Russell Ayto. All rights reserved.
Published by Scholastic Inc., 557 Broadway, New York, NY
10012, by arrangement with HarperCollins Children's Books,
a division of HarperCollins Publishers. SCHOLASTIC and
associated logos are trademarks and/or registered trademarks
of Scholastic Inc.
12 11 10 9 8 7 6   9 10 11 12 13 14/0
Printed in the U.S.A.   40
First Scholastic printing,
April 2009

The Cow That Laid an Egg

SCHOLASTIC INC.
New York Toronto London Auckland Sydney
Mexico City New Delhi Hong Kong Buenos Aires

by Andy Cutbill

illustrated by Russell Ayto

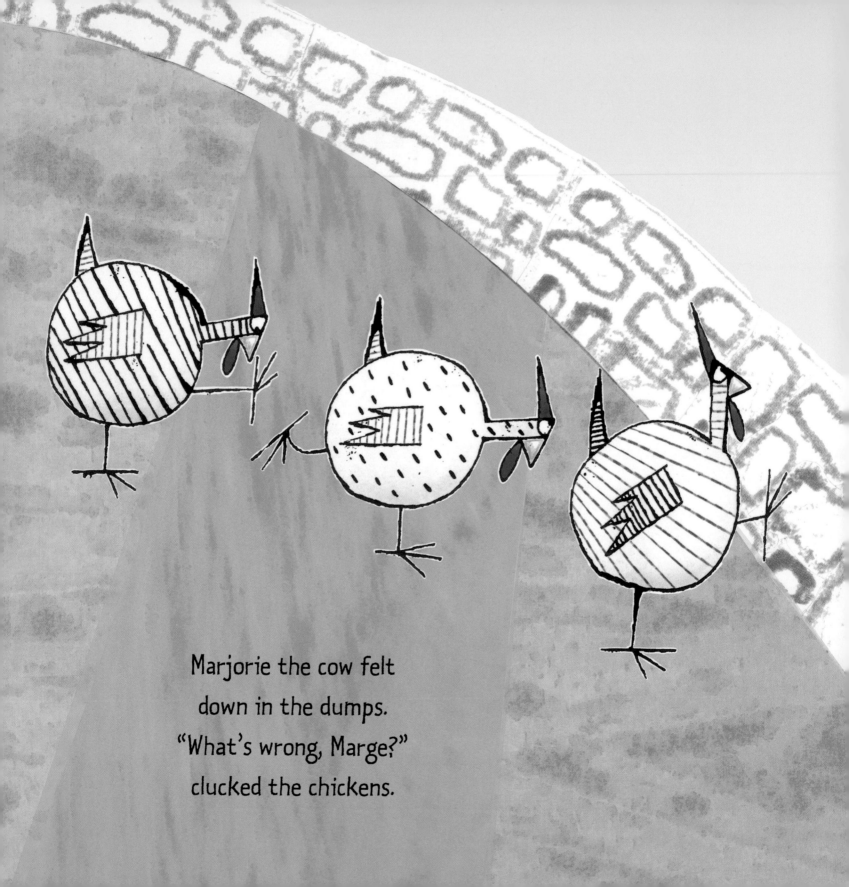

Marjorie the cow felt
down in the dumps.
"What's wrong, Marge?"
clucked the chickens.

"I don't feel special,"
said Marjorie.
"I can't ride bicycles
and do handstands
like the other cows.
I just feel so ordinary."

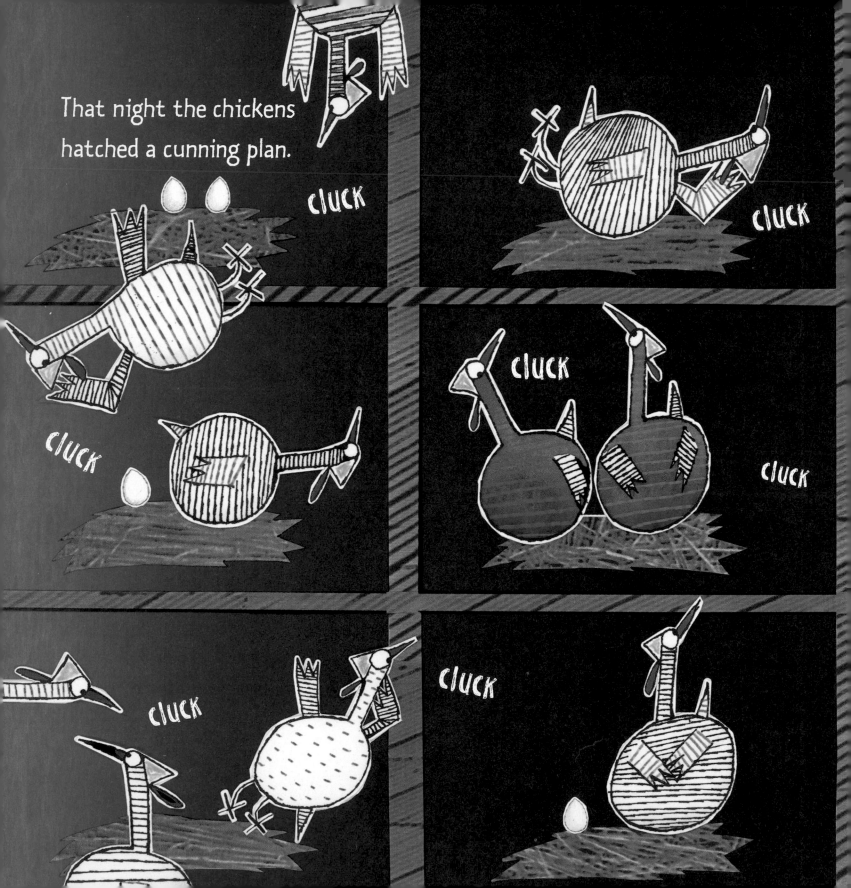

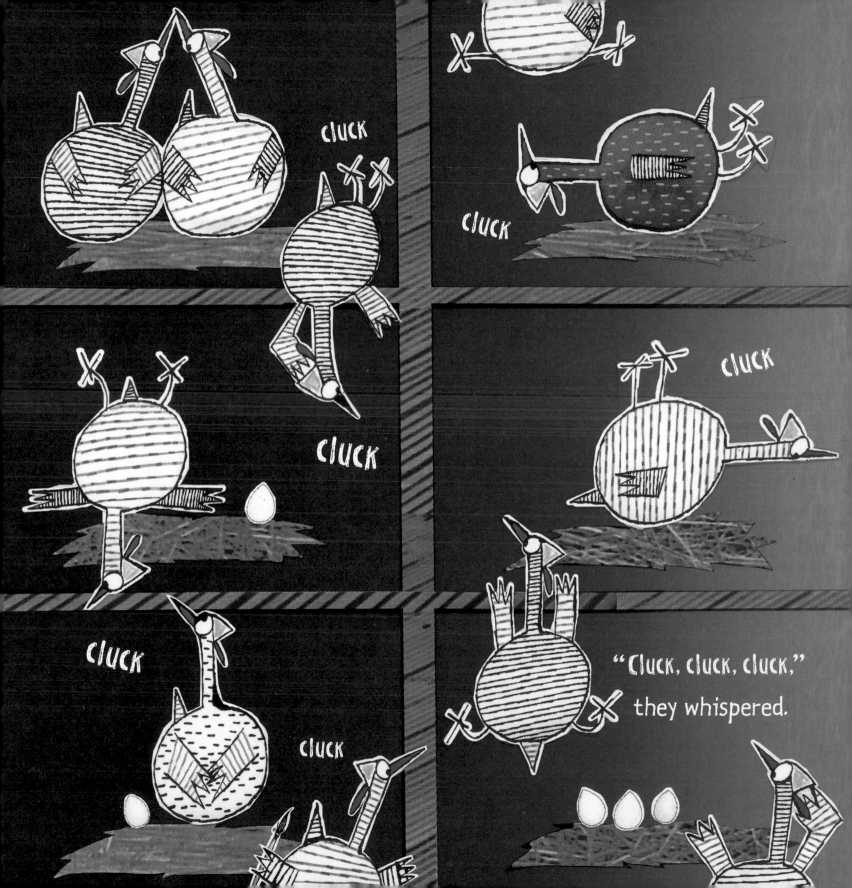

The following morning
there was an almighty commotion
in the barnyard.

"I've laid an egg!"

shrieked Marjorie.

All the other cows
were astonished.
None of them had ever
laid an egg before.

Even the farmer came running. "Oh, my goodness!" he cried. "Marjorie's laid an egg!"

The farmer's wife called the local newspaper.

People came
from far and wide.

"We're extremely proud of Marjorie," announced the farmer to the crowd.

Marjorie felt much
more special now.
And the chickens were
as pleased as Punch too.

But the other cows weren't so happy.

"We don't think you
laid that egg,"
the cows said to Marjorie.
"We think the crafty
chickens did it."

Marjorie felt shocked.

"prove it,"

said the chickens.

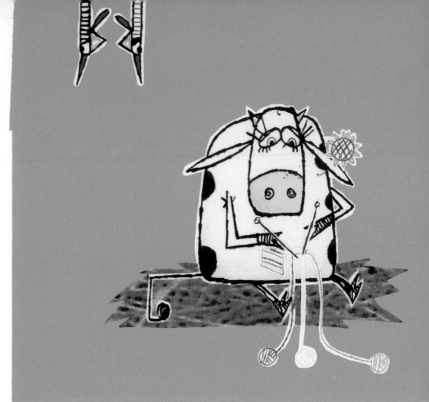

So they all waited for the egg to hatch. Day after day they watched

as Marjorie sat on the egg to keep it warm. But nothing happened.

Until suddenly, one morning,
they heard a noise.

TAP TAP TAP

"Here it comes!" shouted
one of the cows.

And as Marjorie
stood up...

tap tap tap

the egg

cracked

open

and out

hopped

a small, brown,

feathery bundle.

"There," said one of the cows, nodding. "A Chicken!"

Suddenly the tiny
creature looked
up at Marjorie.

OOOOOO!"

it said loudly.

Marjorie smiled and held her baby tight.
"A cow," she said.

And she promptly named it Daisy.